Anton Chekhov,
H.H. Munro (SAKI),
Clara Dillingham Pierson,
Guy de Maupassant,
Hans Christian Andersen,
Oscar Wilde, Banjo Paterson

THE
STUDENT
AND OTHER WRITINGS

DELHI OPEN BOOKS

THE STUDENT
AND OTHER WRITINGS

by Anton Chekhov, H.H. Munro (SAKI),
Clara Dillingham Pierson, Guy de Maupassant,
Hans Christian Andersen, Oscar Wilde, Banjo Paterson

Published by

Delhi Open Books

G/F, 4771/23, Bharat Ram Road, Daryaganj, New Delhi-110002
Ph.: 91-11-42408081
E-mail: **delhiopenbooks2016@gmail.com**

ISBN: 978-81-961623-5-1

Cover, Typesetting, and Book Design by **ROHIT**

Contents

The Student

by Anton Chekhov

At first the weather was fine and still. The thrushes were calling, and in the swamps close by something alive droned pitifully with a sound like blowing into an empty bottle. A snipe flew by, and the shot aimed at it rang out with a gay, resounding note in the spring air. But when it began to get dark in the forest a cold, penetrating wind blew inappropriately from the east, and everything sank into silence. Needles of ice stretched across the pools, and it felt cheerless, remote, and lonely in the forest. There was a whiff of winter.

Ivan Velikopolsky, the son of a sacristan, and a student of the clerical academy, returning home from shooting, kept walking on the path by the water-logged meadows. His fingers were numb and his face was burning with the wind. It seemed to him that the cold that had suddenly come on had destroyed the order and harmony of things, that nature itself felt ill at ease, and that was why the evening darkness was falling more rapidly than usual. All around it was deserted and peculiarly gloomy. The only light was one gleaming in the widows' gardens near the river; the village, over three miles away, and everything in the distance all round was plunged in the cold evening mist. The student remembered that, as he had left the house, his mother was sitting barefoot on the floor in the entryway, cleaning the samovar, while his father lay on the stove coughing; as it was Good Friday nothing had been cooked, and the student was terribly hungry. And now, shrinking from the cold, he thought that just such a wind had blown in the days of Rurik and in the time of Ivan the Terrible and Peter, and in their time there had been just the same desperate poverty and hunger, the same thatched roofs with holes in them, ignorance, misery, the same desolation around, the same darkness, the same feeling of oppression -- all these had existed, did exist, and would exist, and the lapse of a thousand years would make life no better. And he did not want to go home.

The gardens were called the widows' because they were kept by two widows, mother and daughter. A campfire was burning brightly with a crackling sound, throwing out light far around on the ploughed earth. The widow Vasilisa, a tall, fat old woman in a man's coat, was standing by and looking thoughtfully into the fire; her daughter Lukerya, a little pockmarked woman with a stupid-looking face, was sitting on the ground, washing a cauldron and spoons. Apparently they had just had supper. There was a sound of men's voices; it was the laborers watering their horses at the river.

"Here you have winter back again," said the student, going up to the campfire. "Good evening."

Vasilisa started, but at once recognized him and smiled cordially.

"I did not know you; God bless you," she said. "You'll be rich."

They talked. Vasilisa, a woman of experience who had been in service with the gentry, first as a wet-nurse, afterwards as a children's nurse expressed herself with refinement, and a soft, sedate smile never left her face; her daughter Lukerya, a village peasant woman who had been beaten by her husband, simply screwed up her eyes at the student and said nothing, and she had a strange expression like that of a deaf-mute.

"At just such a fire the Apostle Peter warmed himself," said the student, stretching out his hands to the fire, "so it must have been cold then, too. Ah, what a terrible night it must have been, granny! An utterly dismal long night!"

He looked round at the darkness, shook his head abruptly

and asked:

"No doubt you have heard the reading of the Twelve Apostles?"

"Yes, I have," answered Vasilisa.

"If you remember, at the Last Supper Peter said to Jesus, 'I am ready to go with Thee into darkness and unto death.' And our Lord answered him thus: 'I say unto thee, Peter, before the cock croweth thou wilt have denied Me thrice.' After the supper Jesus went through the agony of death in the garden and prayed, and poor Peter was weary in spirit and faint, his eyelids were heavy and he could not struggle against sleep. He fell asleep. Then you heard how Judas the same night kissed Jesus and betrayed Him to His tormentors. They took Him bound to the high priest and beat Him, while Peter, exhausted, worn out with misery and alarm, hardly awake, you know, feeling that something awful was just going to happen on earth, followed behind. . . . He loved Jesus passionately, intensely, and now he saw from far off how He was beaten. . . . "

Lukerya left the spoons and fixed an immovable stare upon the student.

"They came to the high priest's," he went on; "they began to question Jesus, and meantime the laborers made a fire in the yard as it was cold, and warmed themselves. Peter, too, stood with them near the fire and warmed himself as I am doing. A woman, seeing him, said: 'He was with Jesus, too' -- that is as much as to say that he, too, should be taken to be questioned. And all the laborers that were standing near the fire must have looked sourly and suspiciously at him, because he was confused and said: 'I don't know Him.' A little while after again someone recognized him as one of Jesus' disciples and said: 'Thou, too, art one of them,' but again he denied it. And for the third time someone turned to him: 'Why, did I not see thee with Him in the garden today?' For the third time he denied it. And immediately after that time the cock crowed, and Peter, looking from afar off at Jesus, remembered the words He had said to him in the evening. . . . He remembered, he came to himself, went out of the yard and wept bitterly -- bitterly. In the Gospel it is written: 'He went out and wept bitterly.' I imagine it: the still, still, dark, dark garden, and in the stillness, faintly audible, smothered sobbing.. . . ."

The student sighed and sank into thought. Still smiling, Vasilisa suddenly gave a gulp, big tears flowed freely down her cheeks, and she screened her face from the fire with her sleeve as though ashamed of her tears, and Lukerya, staring immovably at the student, flushed crimson, and her expression became strained and heavy like that of someone enduring intense pain.

The laborers came back from the river, and one of them riding a horse was quite near, and the light from the fire quivered upon him. The student said good-night to the widows and went on. And again the darkness was about him and his fingers began to be numb. A cruel wind was blowing, winter really had come back and it did not feel as though Easter would be the day after tomorrow.

Now the student was thinking about Vasilisa: since she had shed tears all that had happened to Peter the night before the Crucifixion must have some relation to her. . . .

He looked round. The solitary light was still gleaming in the darkness and no figures could be seen near it now. The student thought again that if Vasilisa had shed tears, and her daughter had been troubled, it was evident that what he had just been telling them about, which had happened nineteen centuries ago, had a relation to the present -- to both women, to the desolate village, to himself, to all people. The old woman had wept, not because he could tell the story touchingly, but because Peter was near to her, because her whole being was interested in what was passing in Peter's soul.

And joy suddenly stirred in his soul, and he even stopped for a minute to take breath. "The past," he thought, "is linked with the present by an unbroken chain of events flowing one out of another." And it seemed to him that he had just seen both ends of that chain; that when he touched one end the other quivered.

When he crossed the river by the ferryboat and afterwards, mounting the hill, looked at his village and towards the west where the cold crimson sunset lay a narrow streak of light, he thought that truth and beauty which had guided human life there in the garden and in the yard of the high priest had continued without interruption to this day, and had evidently always been the chief thing in human life and in all earthly life, indeed; and the feeling of youth, health, vigor -- he was only twenty-two -- and the inexpressible sweet expectation of happiness, of unknown mysterious happiness, took possession of him little by little, and life seemed to him enchanting, marvellous, and full of lofty meaning.

The Unkindest Blow

by H.H. Munro (SAKI)

The season of strikes seemed to have run itself to a standstill. Almost every trade and industry and calling in which a dislocation could possibly be engineered had indulged in that luxury. The last and least successful convulsion had been the strike of the World's Union of Zoological Garden attendants, who, pending the settlement of certain demands, refused to minister further to the wants of the animals committed to their charge or to allow any other keepers to take their place. In this case the threat of the Zoological Gardens authorities that if the men "came out" the animals should come out also had intensified and precipitated the crisis. The imminent prospect of the larger carnivores, to say nothing of rhinoceroses and bull bison, roaming at large and unfed in the heart of London, was not one which permitted of prolonged conferences. The Government of the day, which from its tendency to be a few hours behind the course of events had been nicknamed the Government of the afternoon, was obliged to intervene with promptitude and decision. A strong force of Bluejackets was despatched to Regent's Park to take over the temporarily abandoned duties of the strikers. Bluejackets were chosen in preference to land forces, partly on account of the traditional readiness of the British Navy to go anywhere and do anything, partly by reason of the familiarity of the average sailor with monkeys, parrots, and other tropical fauna, but chiefly at the urgent request of the First Lord of the Admiralty, who was keenly desirous of an opportunity for performing some personal act of unobtrusive public service within the province of his department.

"If he insists on feeding the infant jaguar himself, in defiance of its mother's wishes, there may be another by-election in the north," said one of his colleagues, with a hopeful inflection in his voice. "By-elections are not very desirable at present, but we must not be selfish."

As a matter of fact the strike collapsed peacefully without any outside intervention. The majority of the keepers had become so attached to their charges that they returned to work of their own accord.

And then the nation and the newspapers turned with a sense of relief to happier things. It seemed as if a new era of contentment was about to dawn. Everybody had struck who could possibly want to strike or who could possibly be cajoled or bullied into striking, whether they wanted to or not. The lighter and brighter side of life might now claim some attention. And conspicuous among the other topics that sprang into sudden prominence was the pending Falvertoon divorce suit.

The Duke of Falvertoon was one of those human hors d'oeuvres that stimulate the public appetite for sensation without giving it much to feed on. As a mere child he had been precociously brilliant; he had declined the editorship of the Anglian Review at an age when most boys are content to have declined Mensa, a table, and though he could not claim to have originated the Futurist movement in literature, his "Letters to a possible Grandson," written at the age of fourteen, had attracted considerable notice. In later days his brilliancy had been less conspicuously displayed. During a debate in the House of Lords on affairs in Morocco, at a moment when that country, for the fifth time in seven years, had brought half Europe to the verge of war, he had interpolated the remark "a little Moor and how much it is," but in spite of the encouraging reception accorded to this one political utterance he was never tempted to a further display in that direction. It began to be generally understood that he did not intend to supplement his numerous town and country residences by living overmuch in the public eye.

And then had come the unlooked-for tidings of the imminent proceedings for divorce. And such a divorce! There were cross-suits and allegations and counter- allegations, charges of cruelty and desertion, everything in fact that was necessary to make the case one of the most complicated and sensational of its kind. And the number of distinguished people involved or cited as witnesses not only embraced both political parties in the realm and several Colonial governors, but included an exotic contingent from France, Hungary, the United States of North America, and the Grand Duchy of Baden. Hotel accommodation of the more expensive sort began to experience a strain on its resources. "It will be quite like the Durbar without the elephants," exclaimed an enthusiastic lady who, to do her justice, had never seen a Durbar. The general feeling was one of thankfulness that the last of the strikes had been got over before the date fixed for the hearing of the great suit.

As a reaction from the season of gloom and industrial strife that had just passed away the agencies that purvey and stage-manage sensations laid themselves out to do their level best on this momentous occasion. Men who had made their reputations as special descriptive writers were mobilised from distant corners of Europe and the further side of the Atlantic in order to enrich with their pens the daily printed records of the case; one word-painter, who specialised in descriptions of how witnesses turn pale under cross-examination, was summoned hurriedly back from a famous and prolonged murder trial in Sicily, where indeed his talents were being decidedly wasted. Thumb-nail artists and expert kodak manipulators were retained at extravagant salaries, and special dress reporters were in high demand. An enterprising Paris firm of costume builders presented the defendant Duchess with three special creations, to be worn, marked, learned, and extensively reported at various critical stages of the trial; and as for the cinematograph agents, their industry and persistence was untiring. Films representing the Duke saying good-bye to his favourite canary on the eve of the trial were in readiness weeks before the event was due to take place; other films depicted the Duchess holding imaginary consultations with fictitious lawyers or making a light repast off specially advertised vegetarian sandwiches during a supposed luncheon interval. As far as human foresight and human enterprise could go nothing was lacking to make the trial a success.

Two days before the case was down for hearing the advance reporter of an important syndicate obtained an interview with the Duke for the purpose of gleaning some final grains of information concerning his Grace's personal arrangements during the trial.

"I suppose I may say this will be one of the biggest affairs of its kind during the lifetime of a generation," began the reporter as an excuse for the unsparing minuteness of detail that he was about to make quest for.

"I suppose so - if it comes off," said the Duke lazily.

"If?" queried the reporter, in a voice that was something between a gasp and a scream.

"The Duchess and I are both thinking of going on strike," said the Duke.

"Strike!"

The baleful word flashed out in all its old hideous familiarity. Was there to be no end to its recurrence?

"Do you mean," faltered the reporter, "that you are contemplating a mutual withdrawal of the charges?"

"Precisely," said the Duke.

"But think of the arrangements that have been made,

the special reporting, the cinematographs, the catering for the distinguished foreign witnesses, the prepared music-hall allusions; think of all the money that has been sunk - "

"Exactly," said the Duke coldly, "the Duchess and I have realised that it is we who provide the material out of which this great far-reaching industry has been built up. Widespread employment will be given and enormous profits made during the duration of the case, and we, on whom all the stress and racket falls, will get - what? An unenviable notoriety and the privilege of paying heavy legal expenses whichever way the verdict goes. Hence our decision to strike. We don't wish to be reconciled; we fully realise that it is a grave step to take, but unless we get some reasonable consideration out of this vast stream of wealth and industry that we have called into being we intend coming out of court and staying out. Good afternoon."

The news of this latest strike spread universal dismay. Its inaccessibility to the ordinary methods of persuasion made it peculiarly formidable. If the Duke and Duchess persisted in being reconciled the Government could hardly be called on to interfere. Public opinion in the shape of social ostracism might be brought to bear on them, but that was as far as coercive measures could go. There was nothing for it but a conference, with powers to propose liberal terms. As it was, several of the foreign witnesses had already departed and others had telegraphed cancelling their hotel arrangements.

The conference, protracted, uncomfortable, and occasionally acrimonious, succeeded at last in arranging for a resumption of litigation, but it was a fruitless victory. The Duke, with a touch of his earlier precocity, died of premature decay a fortnight before the date fixed for the new trial.

The Night Moth With a Crooked Feeler

by Clara Dillingham Pierson

The beautiful, brilliant Butterflies of the Meadow had many cousins living in the forest, most of whom were Night Moths. They also were very beautiful creatures, but they dressed in duller colors and did not have slender waists. Some of the Butterflies, you know, wear whole gowns of black and yellow, others have stripes of black and white, while some have clear yellow with only a bit of black trimming the edges of the wings.

The Moths usually wear brown and have it brightened with touches of buff or dull blue. If they do wear bright colors, it is only on the back pair of wings, and when the Moth alights, he slides his front pair of wings over these and covers all the brightness. They do not rest with their wings folded over their heads like the Butterflies, but leave them flat. All the day long, when the sun is shining, the Moths have to rest on trees and dead leaves. If they were dressed in yellow or red, any passing bird would see them, and there is no telling what might happen. As it is, their brown wings are so nearly the color of dead leaves or bark that you might often look right at them without seeing them.

Yet even among Moths there are some more brightly colored than others, and when you find part of the family quietly dressed you can know it is because they have to lay the eggs. Moths are safer in dull colors, and the egg-layers should always be the safest of all. If anything happened to them, you know, there would be no Caterpillar babies.

One day a fine-looking Cecropia Moth came out of her chrysalis and clung to the nearest twig while her wings grew and dried and flattened. At first they had looked like tiny brown leaves all drenched with rain and wrinkled by somebody's stepping on them. The fur on her fat body was matted and wet, and even her feelers were damp and stuck to her head. Her six beautiful legs were weak and trembling, and she moved her body restlessly while she tried again and again to raise her crumpled wings.

She had not been there so very long before she noticed another Cecropia Moth near her, clinging to the under side of a leaf. He was also just out of the chrysalis and was drying himself. "Good morning!" he cried. "I think I knew you when we were Caterpillars. Fine day to break the chrysalis, isn't it?"

"Lovely," she answered. "I remember you very well. You were the Caterpillar who showed me where to find food last summer when the hot weather had withered so many of the plants."

"I thought you would recall me," he said. "And when we were spinning our chrysalides we visited together. Do you remember that also?"

Miss Cecropia did. She had been thinking of that when she first spoke, but she hoped he had forgotten. To tell the truth, he had been rather fond of her the fall before, and she, thinking him the handsomest Caterpillar of her acquaintance, had smiled upon him and suggested that they spin their cocoons near together. During the long winter she had regretted[Pg 56] this. "I was very foolish," she thought, "to encourage him. When I get my wings I may meet people who are better off than he. Now I shall have to be polite to him for the sake of old friendship. I only hope that he will make other acquaintances and leave me free. I must get into the best society."

All this time her neighbor was thinking, "I am so glad to

see her again, so glad, so glad! When my wings are dry I will fly over to her and we will go through the forest together." He was a kind, warm-hearted fellow, who cared more for friendship than for beauty or family.

Meanwhile their wings were growing fast, and drying, and flattening, so that by noon they could begin to raise them above their heads. They were very large Moths and their wings were of a soft dust color with little clear, transparent places in them and touches of the most beautiful blue, quite the shade worn by the Peacock, who lived on the farm. There was a brown and white border to their wings, and on their bodies and legs the fur was white and dark orange. When the Cecropias rest, they spread their wings out flat, and do not slide the front pair over the others as their cousins, the Sphinxes, do. The most wonderful of all, though, are their feelers.

The Butterflies have stiff feelers on their heads with little knobs on the ends, or sometimes with part of them thick like tiny clubs. The Night Moths have many kinds of feelers, most of them being curved, and those of the Cecropias look like reddish-brown feathers pointed at the end.

Miss Cecropia's feelers were perfect, and she waved them happily to and fro. Those of her friend, she was troubled to see, were not what they should have been. One of them was all right, the other was small and crooked. "Oh dear," she said to herself, "how that does look! I hope he will not try to be attentive to me." He did not mind it much. He thought about other things than looks.

As night came, a Polyphemus Moth fluttered past. "Good evening!" cried he. "Are you just out? There are a lot of Cecropias coming out to-day."

Miss Cecropia felt quite agitated when she heard this, and wondered if she looked all right. Her friend flew over to her just as she raised her wings for flight. "Let me go with you," he said.

While she was wondering how she could answer him, several other Cecropias came along. They were all more brightly colered than she. "Hullo!" cried one of them, as he alighted beside her. "First-rate night, isn't it?"

He was a handsome fellow, and his feelers were perfect; but Miss Cecropia did not like his ways, and she drew away from him just as her friend knocked him off the branch. While they were fighting, another of the strangers flew to her. "May I sit here?" he asked.

"Yes," she murmured, thinking her chance had come to get into society.

"I must say that it served the fellow right for his rudeness to you," said the stranger, in his sweetest way; "but who is the Moth who is punishing him—that queer-looking one with a crooked feeler?"

"Sir," said she, moving farther from him, "he is a friend of mine, and I do not think it matters to you if he is queer-looking."

"Oh!" said the stranger. "Oh! oh! oh! You have a bad temper, haven't you? But you are very good-looking in spite of that." There is no telling what he would have said next, for at this minute Miss Cecropia's friend heard the mean things he was saying, and flew against him.

It was not long before this stranger also was punished, and then the Moth with the crooked feeler turned to the others. "Do any of you want to try it?" he said. "You must understand that you cannot be rude before her." And he pointed his right fore leg at Miss Cecropia as she sat trembling on the branch.

"Her!" they cried mockingly, as they flew away. "There are prettier Moths than she. We don't care anything for her."

Miss Cecropia's friend would have gone after them to

punish them for this impoliteness, but she clung to him and begged him not to. "You will be killed, I know you will," she sobbed. "And then what will become of me?"

"Would you miss me?" he asked, as he felt of one of his wings, now broken and bare.

"Yes," she cried. "You are the best friend I have. Please don't go."

"But I am such a homely fellow," he said. "I don't see how you can like me since I broke my wing.

"Well, I do like you," she said. "Your wing isn't much broken after all, and I like your crooked feeler. It is so different from anybody else's." Miss Cecropia looked very happy as she spoke, and she quite forgot how she once decided to go away from him. There are some people, you know, who can change their minds in such a sweet and easy way that we almost love them the better for it. One certainly could love Miss Cecropia for this, because it showed that she had learned to care more for a warm heart and courage than for whole wings and straight feelers.

Mr. Cecropia did not live long after this, unfortunately, but they were very, very happy together, and she often said to her friends, as she laid her eggs in the best places, "I only hope that when my Caterpillar babies are grown and have come out of their chrysalides, they may be as good and as brave as their father was."

Alexandre

by Guy de Maupassant

At four o'clock that day, as on every other day, Alexandre rolled the three-wheeled chair for cripples up to the door of the little house; then, in obedience to the doctor's orders, he would push his old and infirm mistress about until six o'clock.

When he had placed the light vehicle against the step, just at the place where the old lady could most easily enter it, he went into the house; and soon a furious, hoarse old soldier's voice was heard cursing inside the house: it issued from the master, the retired ex-captain of infantry, Joseph Maramballe.

Then could be heard the noise of doors being slammed, chairs being pushed about, and hasty footsteps; then nothing more. After a few seconds, Alexandre reappeared on the threshold, supporting with all his strength Madame Maramballe, who was exhausted from the exertion of descending the stairs. When she was at last settled in the rolling chair, Alexandre passed behind it, grasped the handle, and set out toward the river.

Thus they crossed the little town every day amid the respectful greeting, of all. These bows were perhaps meant as much for the servant as for the mistress, for if she was loved and esteemed by all, this old trooper, with his long, white, patriarchal beard, was considered a model domestic.

The July sun was beating down unmercifully on the street, bathing the low houses in its crude and burning light. Dogs were sleeping on the sidewalk in the shade of the houses, and Alexandre, a little out of breath, hastened his footsteps in order sooner to arrive at the avenue which leads to the water.

Madame Maramballe was already slumbering under her white parasol, the point of which sometimes grazed along the man's impassive face. As soon as they had reached the Allee des Tilleuls, she awoke in the shade of the trees, and she said in a kindly voice: "Go more slowly, my poor boy; you will kill yourself in this heat."

Along this path, completely covered by arched linden trees, the Mavettek flowed in its winding bed bordered by willows.

The gurgling of the eddies and the splashing of the little waves against the rocks lent to the walk the charming music of babbling water and the freshness of damp air. Madame Maramballe inhaled with deep delight the humid charm of this spot and then murmured: "Ah! I feel better now! But he wasn't in a good humor to-day."

Alexandre answered: "No, madame."

For thirty-five years he had been in the service of this couple, first as officer's orderly, then as simple valet who did not wish to leave his masters; and for the last six years, every afternoon, he had been wheeling his mistress about through the narrow streets of the town. From this long and devoted service, and then from this daily tete-a-tete, a kind of familiarity arose between the old lady and the devoted servant, affectionate on her part, deferential on his.

They talked over the affairs of the house exactly as if they were equals. Their principal subject of conversation and of worry was the bad disposition of the captain, soured by a long career which had begun with promise, run along without promotion, end ended without glory.

Madame Maramballe continued: "He certainly was not in a good humor today. This happens too often since he has left the service."

And Alexandre, with a sigh, completed his mistress's

thoughts, "Oh, madame might say that it happens every day and that it also happened before leaving the army."

"That is true. But the poor man has been so unfortunate. He began with a brave deed, which obtained for him the Legion of Honor at the age of twenty; and then from twenty to fifty he was not able to rise higher than captain, whereas at the beginning he expected to retire with at least the rank of colonel."

"Madame might also admit that it was his fault. If he had not always been as cutting as a whip, his superiors would have loved and protected him better. Harshness is of no use; one should try to please if one wishes to advance. As far as his treatment of us is concerned, it is also our fault, since we are willing to remain with him, but with others it's different."

Madame Maramballe was thinking. Oh, for how many years had she thus been thinking of the brutality of her husband, whom she had married long ago because he was a handsome officer, decorated quite young, and full of promise, so they said! What mistakes one makes in life!

She murmured: "Let us stop a while, my poor Alexandre, and you rest on that bench:

It was a little worm-eaten bench, placed at a turn in the alley. Every time they came in this direction Alexandre was accustomed to making a short pause on this seat.

He sat down and with a proud and familiar gesture he took his beautiful white beard in his hand, and, closing his, fingers over it, ran them down to the point, which he held for a minute at the pit of his stomach, as if once more to verify the length of this growth.

Madame Maramballe continued: "I married him; it is only just and natural that I should bear his injustice; but what I do not understand is why you also should have supported it, my good Alexandre!"

He merely shrugged his shoulders and answered: "Oh! I-- madame."

She added: "Really. I have often wondered. When I married him you were his orderly and you could hardly do otherwise than endure him. But why did you remain with us, who pay you so little and who treat you so badly, when you could have done as every one else does, settle down, marry, have a family?"

He answered: "Oh, madame! with me it's different."

Then he was silent; but he kept pulling his beard as if he were ringing a bell within him, as if he were trying to pull it out, and he rolled his eyes like a man who is greatly embarrassed.

Madame Maramballe was following her own train of thought: "You are not a peasant. You have an education--"

He interrupted her proudly: "I studied surveying, madame."

"Then why did you stay with us, and blast your prospects?"

He stammered: "That's it! that's it! it's the fault of my dispositton."

"How so, of your disposition?"

"Yes, when I become attached to a person I become attached to him, that's all."

She began to laugh: "You are not going to try to tell me that Maramballe's sweet disposition caused you to become attached to him for life."

He was fidgeting about on his bench visibly embarrassed, and he muttered behind his long beard:

"It was not he, it was you!"

The old lady, who had a sweet face, with a snowy line of curly white hair between her forehead and her bonnet, turned around in her chair and observed her servant with a surprised look, exclaiming: "I, my poor Alexandre! How so?"

He began to look up in the air, then to one side, then toward the distance, turning his head as do timid people when forced to admit shameful secrets. At last he exclaimed, with the courage of a trooper who is ordered to the line of fire: "You see, it's this way--the first time I brought a letter to mademoiselle from the lieutenant, mademoiselle gave me a franc and a smile, and that settled it."

Not understanding well, she questioned him "Explain yourself."

Then he cried out, like a malefactor who is admitting a fatal crime: "I had a sentiment for madame! There!"

She answered nothing, stopped looking at him, hung her head, and thought. She was good, full of justice, gentleness, reason, and tenderness. In a second she saw the immense devotion of this poor creature, who had given up everything in order to live beside her, without saying anything. And she felt as if she could cry. Then, with a sad but not angry expression, she said: "Let us return home."

He rose and began to push the wheeled chair.

As they approached the village they saw Captain Maramballe coming toward them. As soon as he joined them he asked his wife, with a visible desire of getting angry: "What have we for dinner?"

"Some chicken with flageolets."

He lost his temper: "Chicken! chicken! always chicken! By all that's holy, I've had enough chicken! Have you no ideas in your head, that you make me eat chicken every day?"

She answered, in a resigned tone: "But, my dear, you know that the doctor has ordered it for you. It's the best thing for your stomach. If your stomach were well, I could give you many things which I do not dare set before you now."

Then, exasperated, he planted himself in front of Alexandre, exclaiming: "Well, if my stomach is out of order it's the fault of that brute. For thirty-five years he has been poisoning me with his abominable cooking."

Madame Maramballe suddenly turned about completely, in order to see the old domestic. Their eyes met, and in this single glance they both said "Thank you!" to each other.

The Thorny Road of Honor

by Hans Christian Andersen

An old story yet lives of the "Thorny Road of Honor," of a marksman, who indeed attained to rank and office, but only after a lifelong and weary strife against difficulties. Who has not, in reading this story, thought of his own strife, and of his own numerous "difficulties?" The story is very closely akin to reality; but still it has its harmonious explanation here on earth, while reality often points beyond the confines of life to the regions of eternity. The history of the world is like a magic lantern that displays to us, in light pictures upon the dark ground of the present, how the benefactors of mankind, the martyrs of genius, wandered along the thorny road of honor.

From all periods, and from every country, these shining pictures display themselves to us. Each only appears for a few moments, but each represents a whole life, sometimes a whole age, with its conflicts and victories. Let us contemplate here and there one of the company of martyrs—the company which will receive new members until the world itself shall pass away.

We look down upon a crowded amphitheatre. Out of the "Clouds" of Aristophanes, satire and humor are pouring down in streams upon the audience; on the stage Socrates, the most remarkable man in Athens, he who had been the shield and defence of the people against the thirty tyrants, is held up mentally and bodily to ridicule—Socrates, who saved Alcibiades and Xenophon in the turmoil of battle, and whose genius soared far above the gods of the ancients. He himself is present; he has risen from the spectator's bench, and has stepped forward, that the laughing Athenians may well appreciate the likeness between himself and the caricature on the stage. There he stands before them, towering high above them all.

Thou juicy, green, poisonous hemlock, throw thy shadow over Athens—not thou, olive tree of fame!

Seven cities contended for the honor of giving birth to Homer—that is to say, they contended after his death! Let us look at him as he was in his lifetime. He wanders on foot through the cities, and recites his verses for a livelihood; the thought for the morrow turns his hair gray! He, the great seer, is blind, and painfully pursues his way—the sharp thorn tears the mantle of the king of poets. His song yet lives, and through that alone live all the heroes and gods of antiquity.

One picture after another springs up from the east, from the west, far removed from each other in time and place, and yet each one forming a portion of the thorny road of honor, on which the thistle indeed displays a flower, but only to adorn the grave.

The camels pass along under the palm trees; they are richly laden with indigo and other treasures of value, sent by the ruler of the land to him whose songs are the delight of the people, the fame of the country. He whom envy and falsehood have driven into exile has been found, and the caravan approaches the little town in which he has taken refuge. A poor corpse is carried out of the town gate, and the funeral procession causes the caravan to halt. The dead man is he whom they have been sent to seek—Firdusi—who has wandered the Thorny road of honor even to the end.

The African, with blunt features, thick lips, and woolly hair, sits on the marble steps of the palace in the capital of Portugal, and begs. He is the submissive slave of Camoens, and but for him, and for the copper coins thrown to him by the passers-by, his master, the poet of the "Lusiad," would die of hunger.

Now, a costly monument marks the grave of Camoens.

There is a new picture.

Behind the iron grating a man appears, pale as death, with long unkempt beard.

"I have made a discovery," he says, "the greatest that has been made for centuries; and they have kept me locked up here for more than twenty years!"

Who is the man?

"A madman," replies the keeper of the madhouse. "What whimsical ideas these lunatics have! He imagines that one can propel things by means of steam."

It is Solomon de Cares, the discoverer of the power of steam, whose theory, expressed in dark words, is not understood by Richelieu; and he dies in the madhouse.

Here stands Columbus, whom the street boys used once to follow and jeer, because he wanted to discover a new world; and he has discovered it. Shouts of joy greet him from the breasts of all, and the clash of bells sounds to celebrate his triumphant return; but the clash of the bells of envy soon drowns the others. The discoverer of a world—he who lifted the American gold land from the sea, and gave it to his king—he is rewarded with iron chains. He wishes that these chains may be placed in his coffin, for they witness to the world of the way in which a man's contemporaries reward good service.

One picture after another comes crowding on; the thorny path of honor and of fame is over-filled.

Here in dark night sits the man who measured the mountains in the moon; he who forced his way out into the endless space, among stars and planets; he, the mighty man who understood the spirit of nature, and felt the earth moving beneath his feet—Galileo. Blind and deaf he sits—an old man thrust through with the spear of suffering, and amid the torments of neglect, scarcely able to lift his foot—that foot with which, in the anguish of his soul, when men denied the truth, he stamped upon the ground, with the exclamation, "Yet it moves!"

Here stands a woman of childlike mind, yet full of faith and inspiration. She carries the banner in front of the combating army, and brings victory and salvation to her fatherland. The sound of shouting arises, and the pile flames up. They are burning the witch, Joan of Arc. Yes, and a future century jeers at the White Lily. Voltaire, the satyr of human intellect, writes "La Pucelle."

At the Thing or Assembly at Viborg, the Danish nobles burn the laws of the king. They flame up high, illuminating the period and the lawgiver, and throw a glory into the dark prison tower, where an old man is growing gray and bent. With his finger he marks out a groove in the stone table. It is the popular king who sits there, once the ruler of three kingdoms, the friend of the citizen and the peasant. It is Christian the Second. Enemies wrote his history. Let us remember his improvements of seven and twenty years, if we cannot forget his crime.

A ship sails away, quitting the Danish shores. A man leans against the mast, casting a last glance towards the Island Hueen. It is Tycho Brahe. He raised the name of Denmark to the stars, and was rewarded with injury, loss and sorrow. He is going to a strange country.

"The vault of heaven is above me everywhere," he says, "and what do I want more?"

And away sails the famous Dane, the astronomer, to live honored and free in a strange land.

"Ay, free, if only from the unbearable sufferings of the body!" comes in a sigh through time, and strikes upon our ear. What a picture! Griffenfeldt, a Danish Prometheus, bound to the rocky island of Munkholm.

We are in America, on the margin of one of the largest rivers; an innumerable crowd has gathered, for it is said that a ship is to sail against the wind and weather, bidding defiance to the elements. The man who thinks he can solve the problem is named Robert Fulton. The ship begins its passage, but suddenly it stops. The crowd begins to laugh and whistle and hiss—the very father of the man whistles with the rest.

"Conceit! Foolery!" is the cry. "It has happened just as he deserved. Put the crack-brain under lock and key!"

Then suddenly a little nail breaks, which had stopped the machine for a few moments; and now the wheels turn again, the floats break the force of the waters, and the ship continues its course; and the beam of the steam engine shortens the distance between far lands from hours into minutes.

O human race, canst thou grasp the happiness of such a minute of consciousness, this penetration of the soul by its mission, the moment in which all dejection, and every wound— even those caused by one's own fault—is changed into health and strength and clearness—when discord is converted to harmony—the minute in which men seem to recognize the manifestation of the heavenly grace in one man, and feel how this one imparts it to all?

Thus the thorny path of honor shows itself as a glory, surrounding the earth with its beams. Thrice happy he who is chosen to be a wanderer there, and, without merit of his own, to be placed between the builder of the bridge and the earth— between Providence and the human race.

On mighty wings the spirit of history floats through the ages, and shows—giving courage and comfort, and awakening gentle thoughts—on the dark nightly background, but in gleaming pictures, the thorny path of honor, which does not, like a fairy tale, end in brilliancy and joy here on earth, but stretches out beyond all time, even into eternity!

The Vendetta

by Guy de Maupassant

The widow of Paolo Saverini lived alone with her son in a poor little house on the outskirts of Bonifacio. The town, built on an outjutting part of the mountain, in places even overhanging the sea, looks across the straits, full of sandbanks, towards the southernmost coast of Sardinia. Beneath it, on the other side and almost surrounding it, is a cleft in the cliff like an immense corridor which serves as a harbor, and along it the little Italian and Sardinian fishing boats come by a circuitous route between precipitous cliffs as far as the first houses, and every two weeks the old, wheezy steamer which makes the trip to Ajaccio.

On the white mountain the houses, massed together, makes an even whiter spot. They look like the nests of wild birds, clinging to this peak, overlooking this terrible passage, where vessels rarely venture. The wind, which blows uninterruptedly, has swept bare the forbidding coast; it drives through the narrow straits and lays waste both sides. The pale streaks of foam, clinging to the black rocks, whose countless peaks rise up out of the water, look like bits of rag floating and drifting on the surface of the sea.

The house of widow Saverini, clinging to the very edge of the precipice, looks out, through its three windows, over this wild and desolate picture.

She lived there alone, with her son Antonia and their dog "Semillante," a big, thin beast, with a long rough coat, of the sheep-dog breed. The young man took her with him when out hunting.

One night, after some kind of a quarrel, Antoine Saverini

was treacherously stabbed by Nicolas Ravolati, who escaped the same evening to Sardinia.

When the old mother received the body of her child, which the neighbors had brought back to her, she did not cry, but she stayed there for a long time motionless, watching him. Then, stretching her wrinkled hand over the body, she promised him a vendetta. She did not wish anybody near her, and she shut herself up beside the body with the dog, which howled continuously, standing at the foot of the bed, her head stretched towards her master and her tail between her legs. She did not move any more than did the mother, who, now leaning over the body with a blank stare, was weeping silently and watching it.

The young man, lying on his back, dressed in his jacket of coarse cloth, torn at the chest, seemed to be asleep. But he had blood all over him; on his shirt, which had been torn off in order to administer the first aid; on his vest, on his trousers, on his face, on his hands. Clots of blood had hardened in his beard and in his hair.

His old mother began to talk to him. At the sound of this voice the dog quieted down.

"Never fear, my boy, my little baby, you shall be avenged. Sleep, sleep; you shall be avenged. Do you hear? It's your mother's promise! And she always keeps her word, your mother does, you know she does."

Slowly she leaned over him, pressing her cold lips to his dead ones.

Then Semillante began to howl again with a long, monotonous, penetrating, horrible howl.

The two of them, the woman and the dog, remained there until morning.

Antoine Saverini was buried the next day and soon his

name ceased to be mentioned in Bonifacio.

He had neither brothers nor cousins. No man was there to carry on the vendetta. His mother, the old woman, alone pondered over it.

On the other side of the straits she saw, from morning until night, a little white speck on the coast. It was the little Sardinian village Longosardo, where Corsican criminals take refuge when they are too closely pursued. They compose almost the entire population of this hamlet, opposite their native island, awaiting the time to return, to go back to the "maquis." She knew that Nicolas Ravolati had sought refuge in this village.

All alone, all day long, seated at her window, she was looking over there and thinking of revenge. How could she do anything without help--she, an invalid and so near death? But she had promised, she had sworn on the body. She could not forget, she could not wait. What could she do? She no longer slept at night; she had neither rest nor peace of mind; she thought persistently. The dog, dozing at her feet, would sometimes lift her head and howl. Since her master's death she often howled thus, as though she were calling him, as though her beast's soul, inconsolable too, had also retained a recollection that nothing could wipe out.

One night, as Semillante began to howl, the mother suddenly got hold of an idea, a savage, vindictive, fierce idea. She thought it over until morning. Then, having arisen at daybreak she went to church. She prayed, prostrate on the floor, begging the Lord to help her, to support her, to give to her poor, broken-down body the strength which she needed in order to avenge her son.

She returned home. In her yard she had an old barrel, which acted as a cistern. She turned it over, emptied it, made it fast to the ground with sticks and stones. Then she chained

Semillante to this improvised kennel and went into the house.

She walked ceaselessly now, her eyes always fixed on the distant coast of Sardinia. He was over there, the murderer.

All day and all night the dog howled. In the morning the old woman brought her some water in a bowl, but nothing more; no soup, no bread.

Another day went by. Semillante, exhausted, was sleeping. The following day her eyes were shining, her hair on end and she was pulling wildly at her chain.

All this day the old woman gave her nothing to eat. The beast, furious, was barking hoarsely. Another night went by.

Then, at daybreak, Mother Saverini asked a neighbor for some straw. She took the old rags which had formerly been worn by her husband and stuffed them so as to make them look like a human body.

Having planted a stick in the ground, in front of Semillante's kennel, she tied to it this dummy, which seemed to be standing up. Then she made a head out of some old rags.

The dog, surprised, was watching this straw man, and was quiet, although famished. Then the old woman went to the store and bought a piece of black sausage. When she got home she started a fire in the yard, near the kennel, and cooked the sausage. Semillante, frantic, was jumping about, frothing at the mouth, her eyes fixed on the food, the odor of which went right to her stomach.

Then the mother made of the smoking sausage a necktie for the dummy. She tied it very tight around the neck with string, and when she had finished she untied the dog.

With one leap the beast jumped at the dummy's throat, and with her paws on its shoulders she began to tear at it. She would fall back with a piece of food in her mouth, then would jump again, sinking her fangs into the string, and snatching few

                    The Student and other writings

pieces of meat she would fall back again and once more spring forward. She was tearing up the face with her teeth and the whole neck was in tatters.

The old woman, motionless and silent, was watching eagerly. Then she chained the beast up again, made her fast for two more days and began this strange performance again.

For three months she accustomed her to this battle, to this meal conquered by a fight. She no longer chained her up, but just pointed to the dummy.

She had taught her to tear him up and to devour him without even leaving any traces in her throat.

Then, as a reward, she would give her a piece of sausage.

As soon as she saw the man, Semillante would begin to tremble. Then she would look up to her mistress, who, lifting her finger, would cry, "Go!" in a shrill tone.

When she thought that the proper time had come, the widow went to confession and, one Sunday morning she partook of communion with an ecstatic fervor. Then, putting on men's clothes and looking like an old tramp, she struck a bargain with a Sardinian fisherman who carried her and her dog to the other side of the straits.

In a bag she had a large piece of sausage. Semillante had had nothing to eat for two days. The old woman kept letting her smell the food and whetting her appetite.

They got to Longosardo. The Corsican woman walked with a limp. She went to a baker's shop and asked for Nicolas Ravolati. He had taken up his old trade, that of carpenter. He was working alone at the back of his store.

The old woman opened the door and called:

"Hallo, Nicolas!"

He turned around. Then releasing her dog, she cried:

"Go, go! Eat him up! eat him up!"

The maddened animal sprang for his throat. The man stretched out his arms, clasped the dog and rolled to the ground. For a few seconds he squirmed, beating the ground with his feet. Then he stopped moving, while Semillante dug her fangs into his throat and tore it to ribbons. Two neighbors, seated before their door, remembered perfectly having seen an old beggar come out with a thin, black dog which was eating something that its master was giving him.

At nightfall the old woman was at home again. She slept well that night.

The Selfish Giant

by Oscar Wilde

Every afternoon, as they were coming from school, the children used to go and play in the Giant's garden.

It was a large lovely garden, with soft green grass. Here and there over the grass stood beautiful flowers like stars, and there were twelve peach-trees that in the spring-time broke out into delicate blossoms of pink and pearl, and in the autumn bore rich fruit. The birds sat on the trees and sang so sweetly that the children used to stop their games in order to listen to them. "How happy we are here!" they cried to each other.

One day the Giant came back. He had been to visit his friend the Cornish ogre, and had stayed with him for seven years. After the seven years were over he had said all that he had to say, for his conversation was limited, and he determined to return to his own castle. When he arrived he saw the children playing in the garden.

"What are you doing here?" he cried in a very gruff voice, and the children ran away.

"My own garden is my own garden," said the Giant; "any one can understand that, and I will allow nobody to play in it but myself." So he built a high wall all round it, and put up a notice-board.

TRESPASSERS

WILL BE

PROSECUTED

He was a very selfish Giant.

The poor children had now nowhere to play. They tried to

play on the road, but the road was very dusty and full of hard stones, and they did not like it. They used to wander round the high wall when their lessons were over, and talk about the beautiful garden inside. "How happy we were there," they said to each other.

Then the Spring came, and all over the country there were little blossoms and little birds. Only in the garden of the Selfish Giant it was still winter. The birds did not care to sing in it as there were no children, and the trees forgot to blossom. Once a beautiful flower put its head out from the grass, but when it saw the notice-board it was so sorry for the children that it slipped back into the ground again, and went off to sleep. The only people who were pleased were the Snow and the Frost. "Spring has forgotten this garden," they cried, "so we will live here all the year round." The Snow covered up the grass with her great white cloak, and the Frost painted all the trees silver. Then they invited the North Wind to stay with them, and he came. He was wrapped in furs, and he roared all day about the garden, and blew the chimney-pots down. "This is a delightful spot," he said, "we must ask the Hail on a visit." So the Hail came. Every day for three hours he rattled on the roof of the castle till he broke most of the slates, and then he ran round and round the garden as fast as he could go. He was dressed in grey, and his breath was like ice.

"I cannot understand why the Spring is so late in coming," said the Selfish Giant, as he sat at the window and looked out at his cold white garden; "I hope there will be a change in the weather."

But the Spring never came, nor the Summer. The Autumn gave golden fruit to every garden, but to the Giant's garden she gave none. "He is too selfish," she said. So it was always Winter there, and the North Wind, and the Hail, and the Frost, and the Snow danced about through the trees.

One morning the Giant was lying awake in bed when he

heard some lovely music. It sounded so sweet to his ears that he thought it must be the King's musicians passing by. It was really only a little linnet singing outside his window, but it was so long since he had heard a bird sing in his garden that it seemed to him to be the most beautiful music in the world. Then the Hail stopped dancing over his head, and the North Wind ceased roaring, and a delicious perfume came to him through the open casement. "I believe the Spring has come at last," said the Giant; and he jumped out of bed and looked out.

What did he see?

He saw a most wonderful sight. Through a little hole in the wall the children had crept in, and they were sitting in the branches of the trees. In every tree that he could see there was a little child. And the trees were so glad to have the children back again that they had covered themselves with blossoms, and were waving their arms gently above the children's heads. The birds were flying about and twittering with delight, and the flowers were looking up through the green grass and laughing. It was a lovely scene, only in one corner it was still winter. It was the farthest corner of the garden, and in it was standing a little boy. He was so small that he could not reach up to the branches of the tree, and he was wandering all round it, crying bitterly. The poor tree was still quite covered with frost and snow, and the North Wind was blowing and roaring above it. "Climb up! little boy," said the Tree, and it bent its branches down as low as it could; but the boy was too tiny.

And the Giant's heart melted as he looked out. "How selfish I have been!" he said; "now I know why the Spring would not come here. I will put that poor little boy on the top of the tree, and then I will knock down the wall, and my garden shall be the children's playground for ever and ever." He was really very sorry for what he had done.

So he crept downstairs and opened the front door quite softly, and went out into the garden. But when the children saw him they were so frightened that they all ran away, and the garden became winter again. Only the little boy did not run, for his eyes were so full of tears that he did not see the Giant coming. And the Giant stole up behind him and took him gently in his hand, and put him up into the tree. And the tree broke at once into blossom, and the birds came and sang on it, and the little boy stretched out his two arms and flung them round the Giant's neck, and kissed him. And the other children, when they saw that the Giant was not wicked any longer, came running back, and with them came the Spring. "It is your garden now, little children," said the Giant, and he took a great axe and knocked down the wall. And when the people were going to market at twelve o'clock they found the Giant playing with the children in the most beautiful garden they had ever seen.

All day long they played, and in the evening they came to the Giant to bid him good-bye.

"But where is your little companion?" he said: "the boy I put into the tree." The Giant loved him the best because he had kissed him.

"We don't know," answered the children; "he has gone away."

"You must tell him to be sure and come here to-morrow," said the Giant. But the children said that they did not know where he lived, and had never seen him before; and the Giant felt very sad.

Every afternoon, when school was over, the children came and played with the Giant. But the little boy whom the Giant loved was never seen again. The Giant was very kind to all the children, yet he longed for his first little friend, and often spoke of him. "How I would like to see him!" he used to say.

Years went over, and the Giant grew very old and feeble. He could not play about any more, so he sat in a huge armchair, and watched the children at their games, and admired his garden. "I have many beautiful flowers," he said; "but the children are the most beautiful flowers of all."

One winter morning he looked out of his window as he was dressing. He did not hate the Winter now, for he knew that it was merely the Spring asleep, and that the flowers were resting.

Suddenly he rubbed his eyes in wonder, and looked and looked. It certainly was a marvellous sight. In the farthest corner of the garden was a tree quite covered with lovely white blossoms. Its branches were all golden, and silver fruit hung down from them, and underneath it stood the little boy he had loved.

Downstairs ran the Giant in great joy, and out into the garden. He hastened across the grass, and came near to the child. And when he came quite close his face grew red with anger, and he said, "Who hath dared to wound thee?" For on the palms of the child's hands were the prints of two nails, and the prints of two nails were on the little feet.

"Who hath dared to wound thee?" cried the Giant; "tell me, that I may take my big sword and slay him."

"Nay!" answered the child; "but these are the wounds of Love."

"Who art thou?" said the Giant, and a strange awe fell on him, and he knelt before the little child.

And the child smiled on the Giant, and said to him, "You let me play once in your garden, to-day you shall come with me to my garden, which is Paradise."

And when the children ran in that afternoon, they found the Giant lying dead under the tree, all covered with white blossoms.

The Looking Glass

by Anton Chekhov

NEW YEAR'S EVE. Nellie, the daughter of a landowner and general, a young and pretty girl, dreaming day and night of being married, was sitting in her room, gazing with exhausted, half-closed eyes into the looking-glass. She was pale, tense, and as motionless as the looking-glass.

The non-existent but apparent vista of a long, narrow corridor with endless rows of candles, the reflection of her face, her hands, of the frame -- all this was already clouded in mist and merged into a boundless grey sea. The sea was undulating, gleaming and now and then flaring crimson. . . .

Looking at Nellie's motionless eyes and parted lips, one could hardly say whether she was asleep or awake, but nevertheless she was seeing. At first she saw only the smile and soft, charming expression of someone's eyes, then against the shifting grey background there gradually appeared the outlines of a head, a face, eyebrows, beard. It was he, the destined one, the object of long dreams and hopes. The destined one was for Nellie everything, the significance of life, personal happiness, career, fate. Outside him, as on the grey background of the looking-glass, all was dark, empty, meaningless. And so it was not strange that, seeing before her a handsome, gently smiling face, she was conscious of bliss, of an unutterably sweet dream that could not be expressed in speech or on paper. Then she heard his voice, saw herself living under the same roof with him, her life merged into his. Months and years flew by against the grey background. And Nellie saw her future distinctly in all its details.

Picture followed picture against the grey background. Now

    The Student and other writings

Nellie saw herself one winter night knocking at the door of Stepan Lukitch, the district doctor. The old dog hoarsely and lazily barked behind the gate. The doctor's windows were in darkness. All was silence.

"For God's sake, for God's sake!" whispered Nellie.

But at last the garden gate creaked and Nellie saw the doctor's cook.

"Is the doctor at home?"

"His honour's asleep," whispered the cook into her sleeve, as though afraid of waking her master.

"He's only just got home from his fever patients, and gave orders he was not to be waked."

But Nellie scarcely heard the cook. Thrusting her aside, she rushed headlong into the doctor's house. Running through some dark and stuffy rooms, upsetting two or three chairs, she at last reached the doctor's bedroom. Stepan Lukitch was lying on his bed, dressed, but without his coat, and with pouting lips was breathing into his open hand. A little night-light glimmered faintly beside him. Without uttering a word Nellie sat down and began to cry. She wept bitterly, shaking all over.

"My husband is ill!" she sobbed out. Stepan Lukitch was silent. He slowly sat up, propped his head on his hand, and looked at his visitor with fixed, sleepy eyes. "My husband is ill!" Nellie continued, restraining her sobs. "For mercy's sake come quickly. Make haste. . . . Make haste!"

"Eh?" growled the doctor, blowing into his hand.

"Come! Come this very minute! Or . . . it's terrible to think! For mercy's sake!"

And pale, exhausted Nellie, gasping and swallowing her tears, began describing to the doctor her husband's illness, her unutterable terror. Her sufferings would have touched the heart of a stone, but the doctor looked at her, blew into his open hand, and -- not a movement.

"I'll come to-morrow!" he muttered.

"That's impossible!" cried Nellie. "I know my husband has typhus! At once . . . this very minute you are needed!"

"I . . . er . . . have only just come in," muttered the doctor. "For the last three days I've been away, seeing typhus patients, and I'm exhausted and ill myself. . . . I simply can't! Absolutely! I've caught it myself! There!"

And the doctor thrust before her eyes a clinical thermometer.

"My temperature is nearly forty. . . . I absolutely can't. I can scarcely sit up. Excuse me. I'll lie down. . . ."

The doctor lay down.

"But I implore you, doctor," Nellie moaned in despair. "I beseech you! Help me, for mercy's sake! Make a great effort and come! I will repay you, doctor!"

"Oh, dear! . . . Why, I have told you already. Ah!"

Nellie leapt up and walked nervously up and down the bedroom. She longed to explain to the doctor, to bring him to reason. . . . She thought if only he knew how dear her husband was to her and how unhappy she was, he would forget his exhaustion and his illness. But how could she be eloquent enough?

"Go to the Zemstvo doctor," she heard Stepan Lukitch's voice.

"That's impossible! He lives more than twenty miles from here, and time is precious. And the horses can't stand it. It is thirty miles from us to you, and as much from here to the Zemstvo doctor. No, it's impossible! Come along, Stepan Lukitch. I ask of you an heroic deed. Come, perform that heroic deed! Have pity on us!"

"It's beyond everything. . . . I'm in a fever. . . my head's in a whirl . . . and she won't understand! Leave me alone!"

"But you are in duty bound to come! You cannot refuse to come! It's egoism! A man is bound to sacrifice his life for his neighbour, and you. . . you refuse to come! I will summon you before the Court."

Nellie felt that she was uttering a false and undeserved insult, but for her husband's sake she was capable of forgetting logic, tact, sympathy for others. . . . In reply to her threats, the doctor greedily gulped a glass of cold water. Nellie fell to entreating and imploring like the very lowest beggar. . . . At last the doctor gave way. He slowly got up, puffing and panting, looking for his coat.

"Here it is!" cried Nellie, helping him. "Let me put it on to you. Come along! I will repay you. . . . All my life I shall be grateful to you. . . ."

But what agony! After putting on his coat the doctor lay down again. Nellie got him up and dragged him to the hall. Then there was an agonizing to-do over his goloshes, his overcoat. . . . His cap was lost. . . . But at last Nellie was in the carriage with the doctor. Now they had only to drive thirty miles and her husband would have a doctor's help. The earth was wrapped in darkness. One could not see one's hand before one's face. . . . A cold winter wind was blowing. There were frozen lumps under their wheels. The coachman was continually stopping and wondering which road to take.

Nellie and the doctor sat silent all the way. It was fearfully jolting, but they felt neither the cold nor the jolts.

"Get on, get on!" Nellie implored the driver.

At five in the morning the exhausted horses drove into the yard. Nellie saw the familiar gates, the well with the crane, the long row of stables and barns. At last she was at home.

"Wait a moment, I will be back directly," she said to Stepan Lukitch, making him sit down on the sofa in the dining-room. "Sit still and wait a little, and I'll see how he is going on."

On her return from her husband, Nellie found the doctor lying down. He was lying on the sofa and muttering.

"Doctor, please! . . . doctor!"

"Eh? Ask Domna!" muttered Stepan Lukitch.

"What?"

"They said at the meeting . . . Vlassov said . . . Who? . . . what?"

And to her horror Nellie saw that the doctor was as delirious as her husband. What was to be done?

"I must go for the Zemstvo doctor," she decided.

Then again there followed darkness, a cutting cold wind, lumps of frozen earth. She was suffering in body and in soul, and delusive nature has no arts, no deceptions to compensate these sufferings. . . .

Then she saw against the grey background how her husband every spring was in straits for money to pay the interest for the mortgage to the bank. He could not sleep, she could not sleep, and both racked their brains till their heads ached, thinking how to avoid being visited by the clerk of the Court.

She saw her children: the everlasting apprehension of colds, scarlet fever, diphtheria, bad marks at school, separation. Out of a brood of five or six one was sure to die.

The grey background was not untouched by death. That might well be. A husband and wife cannot die simultaneously. Whatever happened one must bury the other. And Nellie saw her husband dying. This terrible event presented itself to her in every detail. She saw the coffin, the candles, the deacon, and even the footmarks in the hall made by the undertaker.

"Why is it, what is it for?" she asked, looking blankly at her husband's face.

And all the previous life with her husband seemed to her a stupid prelude to this.

Something fell from Nellie's hand and knocked on the floor. She started, jumped up, and opened her eyes wide. One looking-glass she saw lying at her feet. The other was standing as before on the table.

She looked into the looking-glass and saw a pale, tear-stained face. There was no grey background now.

"I must have fallen asleep," she thought with a sigh of relief.

Vanka

by Anton Chekhov

VANKA ZHUKOV, a boy of nine, who had been for three months apprenticed to Alyahin the shoemaker, was sitting up on Christmas Eve. Waiting till his master and mistress and their workmen had gone to the midnight service, he took out of his master's cupboard a bottle of ink and a pen with a rusty nib, and, spreading out a crumpled sheet of paper in front of him, began writing. Before forming the first letter he several times looked round fearfully at the door and the windows, stole a glance at the dark ikon, on both sides of which stretched shelves full of lasts, and heaved a broken sigh. The paper lay on the bench while he knelt before it.

"Dear grandfather, Konstantin Makaritch," he wrote, "I am writing you a letter. I wish you a happy Christmas, and all blessings from God Almighty. I have neither father nor mother, you are the only one left me."

Vanka raised his eyes to the dark ikon on which the light of his candle was reflected, and vividly recalled his grandfather, Konstantin Makaritch, who was night watchman to a family called Zhivarev. He was a thin but extraordinarily nimble and lively little old man of sixty-five, with an everlastingly laughing face and drunken eyes. By day he slept in the servants' kitchen, or made jokes with the cooks; at night, wrapped in an ample sheepskin, he walked round the grounds and tapped with his little mallet. Old Kashtanka and Eel, so-called on account of his dark colour and his long body like a weasel's, followed him with hanging heads. This Eel was exceptionally polite and affectionate, and looked with equal kindness on strangers and his own masters, but had not a very good reputation. Under his politeness and meekness was hidden the most Jesuitical cunning. No one knew better how to creep up on occasion and snap at one's legs, to slip into the store-room, or steal a hen from a peasant. His hind legs had been nearly pulled off more than once, twice he had been hanged, every week he was thrashed till he was half dead, but he always revived.

At this moment grandfather was, no doubt, standing at the gate, screwing up his eyes at the red windows of the church, stamping with his high felt boots, and joking with the servants. His little mallet was hanging on his belt. He was clasping his hands, shrugging with the cold, and, with an aged chuckle, pinching first the housemaid, then the cook.

"How about a pinch of snuff?" he was saying, offering the women his snuff-box.

The women would take a sniff and sneeze. Grandfather would be indescribably delighted, go off into a merry chuckle, and cry:

"Tear it off, it has frozen on!"

They give the dogs a sniff of snuff too. Kashtanka sneezes, wriggles her head, and walks away offended. Eel does not sneeze, from politeness, but wags his tail. And the weather is glorious. The air is still, fresh, and transparent. The night is dark, but one can see the whole village with its white roofs and coils of smoke coming from the chimneys, the trees silvered with hoar frost, the snowdrifts. The whole sky spangled with gay twinkling stars, and the Milky Way is as distinct as though it had been washed and rubbed with snow for a holiday. . . .

Vanka sighed, dipped his pen, and went on writing:

"And yesterday I had a wigging. The master pulled me out into the yard by my hair, and whacked me with a boot-stretcher because I accidentally fell asleep while I was rocking their brat in the cradle. And a week ago the mistress told me to clean a herring, and I began from the tail end, and she took the herring and thrust its head in my face. The workmen laugh at me and send me to the tavern for vodka, and tell me to steal the master's cucumbers for them, and the master beats me with anything that comes to hand. And there is nothing to eat. In the morning they give me bread, for dinner, porridge, and in the evening, bread again; but as for tea, or soup, the master and mistress gobble it all up themselves. And I am put to sleep in the passage, and when their wretched brat cries I get no sleep at all, but have to rock the cradle. Dear grandfather, show the divine mercy, take me away from here, home to the village. It's more than I can bear. I bow down to your feet, and will pray to God for you for ever, take me away from here or I shall die."

Vanka's mouth worked, he rubbed his eyes with his black fist, and gave a sob.

"I will powder your snuff for you," he went on. "I will pray for you, and if I do anything you can thrash me like Sidor's goat. And if you think I've no job, then I will beg the steward for Christ's sake to let me clean his boots, or I'll go for a shepherd-boy instead of Fedka. Dear grandfather, it is more than I can bear, it's simply no life at all. I wanted to run away to the village, but I have no boots, and I am afraid of the frost. When I grow up big I will take care of you for this, and not let anyone annoy you, and when you die I will pray for the rest of your soul, just as for my mammy's.

Moscow is a big town. It's all gentlemen's houses, and there are lots of horses, but there are no sheep, and the dogs are not spiteful. The lads here don't go out with the star, and they don't let anyone go into the choir, and once I saw in a shop window fishing-hooks for sale, fitted ready with the line and for all sorts of fish, awfully good ones, there was even one hook that would hold a forty-pound sheat-fish. And I have seen shops where there are guns of all sorts, after the pattern of the master's guns at home, so that I shouldn't wonder if they are a hundred roubles each. . . . And in the butchers' shops there are grouse and woodcocks and fish and hares, but the shopmen don't say where they shoot them.

"Dear grandfather, when they have the Christmas tree at the big house, get me a gilt walnut, and put it away in the green trunk. Ask the young lady Olga Ignatyevna, say it's for Vanka."

Vanka gave a tremulous sigh, and again stared at the window. He remembered how his grandfather always went into the forest to get the Christmas tree for his master's family, and took his grandson with him. It was a merry time! Grandfather made a noise in his throat, the forest crackled with the frost, and looking at them Vanka chortled too. Before chopping down the Christmas tree, grandfather would smoke a pipe, slowly take a pinch of snuff, and laugh at frozen Vanka. . . . The young fir trees, covered with hoar frost, stood motionless, waiting to see which of them was to die. Wherever one looked, a hare flew like an arrow over the snowdrifts. . . . Grandfather could not refrain from shouting: "Hold him, hold him . . . hold him! Ah, the bob-tailed devil!"

When he had cut down the Christmas tree, grandfather used to drag it to the big house, and there set to work to decorate it. . . . The young lady, who was Vanka's favourite, Olga Ignatyevna, was the busiest of all. When Vanka's mother Pelageya was alive, and a servant in the big house, Olga Ignatyevna used to give him goodies, and having nothing better to do, taught him to read and write, to count up to a hundred, and even to dance a quadrille. When Pelageya died, Vanka had been transferred to the servants' kitchen to be with his grandfather, and from the kitchen to the shoemaker's in Moscow.

"Do come, dear grandfather," Vanka went on with his letter. "For Christ's sake, I beg you, take me away. Have pity on an unhappy orphan like me; here everyone knocks me about, and I am fearfully hungry; I can't tell you what misery it is, I am always crying. And the other day the master hit me on the head with a last, so that I fell down. My life is wretched, worse than any dog's. . . . I send greetings to Alyona, one-eyed Yegorka, and the coachman, and don't give my concertina to anyone. I remain, your grandson, Ivan Zhukov. Dear grandfather, do come."

Vanka folded the sheet of writing-paper twice, and put it into an envelope he had bought the day before for a kopeck. . . . After thinking a little, he dipped the pen and wrote the address:

To grandfather in the village.

Then he scratched his head, thought a little, and added: Konstantin Makaritch. Glad that he had not been prevented from writing, he put on his cap and, without putting on his little greatcoat, ran out into the street as he was in his shirt. . . .

The shopmen at the butcher's, whom he had questioned the day before, told him that letters were put in post-boxes, and from the boxes were carried about all over the earth in mailcarts with drunken drivers and ringing bells. Vanka ran to the nearest post-box, and thrust the precious letter in the slit. . . .

An hour later, lulled by sweet hopes, he was sound asleep. . . . He dreamed of the stove. On the stove was sitting his grandfather, swinging his bare legs, and reading the letter to the cooks. . . .

By the stove was Eel, wagging his tail.

The Merino Sheep

by Banjo Paterson

People have got the impression that the merino is a gentle, bleating animal that gets its living without trouble to anybody, and comes up every year to be shorn with a pleased smile upon its amiable face. It is my purpose here to exhibit the merino sheep in its true light.

First let us give him his due. No one can accuse him of being a ferocious animal. No one could ever say that a sheep attacked him without provocation; although there is an old bush story of a man who was discovered in the act of killing a neighbour's wether.

"Hello!" said the neighbour, "What's this? Killing my sheep! What have you got to say for yourself?"

"Yes," said the man, with an air of virtuous indignation. "I AM killing your sheep. I'll kill ANY man's sheep that bites ME!"

But as a rule the merino refrains from using his teeth on people. He goes to work in another way.

The truth is that he is a dangerous monomaniac, and his one idea is to ruin the man who owns him. With this object in view he will display a talent for getting into trouble and a genius for dying that are almost incredible.

If a mob of sheep see a bush fire closing round them, do they run away out of danger? Not at all, they rush round and round in a ring till the fire burns them up. If they are in a river-bed, with a howling flood coming down, they will stubbornly refuse to cross three inches of water to save themselves. Dogs may bark and men may shriek, but the sheep won't move. They will wait there till the flood comes and drowns them all, and then their corpses go down the river on their backs with their feet in the air.

A mob will crawl along a road slowly enough to exasperate a snail, but let a lamb get away in a bit of rough country, and a racehorse can't head him back again. If sheep are put into a big paddock with water in three corners of it, they will resolutely crowd into the fourth, and die of thirst.

When being counted out at a gate, if a scrap of bark be left on the ground in the gateway, they will refuse to step over it until dogs and men have sweated and toiled and sworn and "heeled 'em up", and "spoke to 'em", and fairly jammed them at it. At last one will gather courage, rush at the fancied obstacle, spring over it about six feet in the air, and dart away. The next does exactly the same, but jumps a bit higher. Then comes a rush of them following one another in wild bounds like antelopes, until one overjumps himself and alights on his head. This frightens those still in the yard, and they stop running out.

Then the dogging and shrieking and hustling and tearing have to be gone through all over again. (This on a red-hot day, mind you, with clouds of blinding dust about, the yolk of wool irritating your eyes, and, perhaps, three or four thousand sheep to put through). The delay throws out the man who is counting, and he forgets whether he left off at 45 or 95. The dogs, meanwhile, have taken the first chance to slip over the fence and hide in the shade somewhere, and then there are loud whistlings and oaths, and calls for Rover and Bluey. At last a dirt-begrimed man jumps over the fence, unearths Bluey, and hauls him back by the ear. Bluey sets to work barking and heeling-'em up again, and pretends that he thoroughly enjoys it; but all the while he is looking out for another chance to "clear". And THIS time he won't be discovered in a hurry.

There is a well-authenticated story of a ship-load of sheep

that was lost because an old ram jumped overboard, and all the rest followed him. No doubt they did, and were proud to do it. A sheep won't go through an open gate on his own responsibility, but he would gladly and proudly "follow the leader" through the red-hot portals of Hades: and it makes no difference whether the lead goes voluntarily, or is hauled struggling and kicking and fighting every inch of the way.

For pure, sodden stupidity there is no animal like the merino. A lamb will follow a bullock-dray, drawn by sixteen bullocks and driven by a profane person with a whip, under the impression that the aggregate monstrosity is his mother. A ewe never knows her own lamb by sight, and apparently has no sense of colour. She can recognise its voice half a mile off among a thousand other voices apparently exactly similar; but when she gets within five yards of it she starts to smell all the other lambs within reach, including the black ones -- though her own may be white.

The fiendish resemblance which one sheep bears to another is a great advantage to them in their struggles with their owners. It makes it more difficult to draft them out of a strange flock, and much harder to tell when any are missing.

Concerning this resemblance between sheep, there is a story told of a fat old Murrumbidgee squatter who gave a big price for a famous ram called Sir Oliver. He took a friend out one day to inspect Sir Oliver, and overhauled that animal with a most impressive air of sheep-wisdom.

"Look here," he said, "at the fineness of the wool. See the serrations in each thread of it. See the density of it. Look at the way his legs and belly are clothed -- he's wool all over, that sheep. Grand animal, grand animal!"

Then they went and had a drink, and the old squatter said, "Now, I'll show you the difference between a champion ram and a second-rater." So he caught a ram and pointed out his defects. "See here -- not half the serrations that other sheep had. No density of fleece to speak of. Bare-bellied as a pig, compared with Sir Oliver. Not that this isn't a fair sheep, but he'd be dear at one-tenth Sir Oliver's price. By the way, Johnson" (to his overseer), "what ram IS this?"

"That, sir," replied the astounded functionary -- "that IS Sir Oliver, sir!"

There is another kind of sheep in Australia, as great a curse in his own way as the merino -- namely, the cross-bred, or half-merino-half-Leicester animal. The cross-bred will get through, under, or over any fence you like to put in front of him. He is never satisfied with his owner's run, but always thinks other people's runs must be better, so he sets off to explore. He will strike a course, say, south-east, and so long as the fit takes him he will keep going south-east through all obstacles -- rivers, fences, growing crops, anything. The merino relies on passive resistance for his success; the cross-bred carries the war into the enemy's camp, and becomes a living curse to his owner day and night.

Once there was a man who was induced in a weak moment to buy twenty cross-bred rams. From that hour the hand of Fate was upon him. They got into all the paddocks they shouldn't have been in. They scattered themselves over the run promiscuously. They visited the cultivation paddock and the vegetable-garden at their own sweet will. And then they took to roving. In a body they visited the neighbouring stations, and played havoc with the sheep all over the district.

The wretched owner was constantly getting fiery letters from his neighbours: "Your blanky rams are here. Come and take them away at once," and he would have to go nine or ten miles to drive them home. Any man who has tried to drive rams on a hot day knows what purgatory is. He was threatened every week with actions for trespass.

He tried shutting them up in the sheep-yard. They got out

                    The Student and other writings

and went back to the garden. Then he gaoled them in the calf-pen. Out again and into a growing crop. Then he set a boy to watch them; but the boy went to sleep, and they were four miles away across country before he got on to their tracks.

At length, when they happened accidentally to be at home on their owner's run, there came a big flood. His sheep, mostly merinos, had plenty of time to get on to high ground and save their lives; but, of course, they didn't, and were almost all drowned. The owner sat on a rise above the waste of waters and watched the dead animals go by. He was a ruined man. But he said, "Thank God, those cross-bred rams are drowned, anyhow." Just as he spoke there was a splashing in the water, and the twenty rams solemnly swam ashore and ranged themselves in front of him. They were the only survivors of his twenty thousand sheep. He broke down, and was taken to an asylum for insane paupers. The cross-breds had fulfilled their destiny.

The cross-bred drives his owner out of his mind, but the merino ruins his man with greater celerity. Nothing on earth will kill cross-breds; nothing will keep merinos alive. If they are put on dry salt-bush country they die of drought. If they are put on damp, well-watered country they die of worms, fluke, and foot-rot. They die in the wet seasons and they die in the dry ones.

The hard, resentful look on the faces of all bushmen comes from a long course of dealing with merino sheep. The merino dominates the bush, and gives to Australian literature its melancholy tinge, its despairing pathos. The poems about dying boundary-riders, and lonely graves under mournful she-oaks, are the direct outcome of the poet's too close association with that soul-destroying animal. A man who could write anything cheerful after a day in the drafting-yards would be a freak of nature.